iRℓs

a
pinch of
magic

Written by
Kiki Thorpe

Illustrated by
Jana Christy

A STEPPING STONE BOOK™
RANDOM HOUSE 🏠 NEW YORK

For Oonagh
—K.T.

For my sister, Angela
—J.C.

Library of Congress Cataloging-in-Publication Data
Thorpe, Kiki.
A pinch of magic / written by Kiki Thorpe ; illustrated by Jana Christy.
pages cm — (The Never girls ; 7)
"A Stepping Stone book."
Summary: Baking-talent fairy Dulcie helps Mia make treats for a neighborhood bake
sale but must return to Never Land before they are done, and Mia may not be able to
finish without her help.
ISBN 978-0-7364-3097-5 (trade) — ISBN 978-0-7364-8149-6 (lib. bdg.) —
ISBN 978-0-7364-3222-1 (ebook)
[1. Fairies—Fiction. 2. Magic—Fiction. 3. Baking—Fiction. 4. Contests—Fiction.]
I. Title.
PZ7.T3974Pin 2014
[Fic]—dc23
2014004047

randomhouse.com/kids/disney
Printed in the United States of America
10 9 8 7 6 5 4 3 2

Never Land

Far away from the world we know, on the distant seas of dreams, lies an island called Never Land. It is a place full of magic, where mermaids sing, fairies play, and children never grow up. Adventures happen every day, and anything is possible.

There are two ways to reach Never Land. One is to find the island yourself. The other is for it to find you. Finding Never Land on your own takes a lot of luck and a pinch of fairy dust. Even then, you will only find the island if it wants to be found.

Every once in a while, Never Land drifts close to our world . . . so close a fairy's laugh slips through. And every once in an even longer while, Never Land opens its doors to a special few. Believing in magic and fairies from the bottom of your heart can make the extraordinary happen. If you suddenly hear tiny bells or feel a sea breeze where there is no sea, pay careful attention. Never Land may be close by. You could find yourself there in the blink of an eye.

One day, four special girls came to Never Land in just this way. This is their story.

Never Land

Pirate Cove

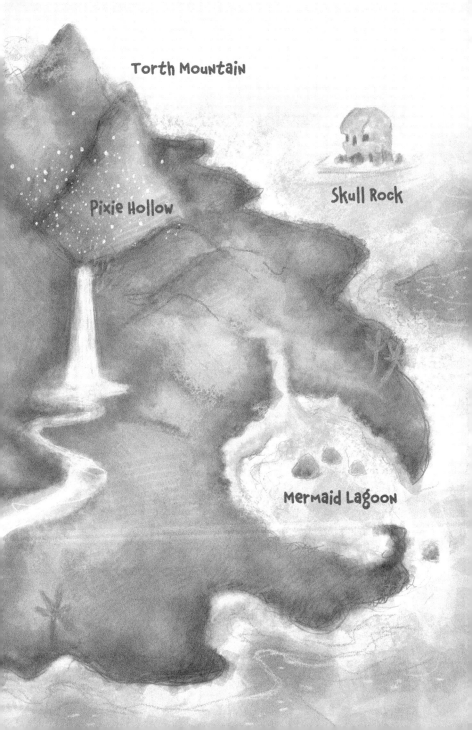

Torth Mountain

Skull Rock

Pixie Hollow

Mermaid Lagoon

Chapter 1

"Last one home is a rotten egg!" cried Gabby Vasquez. She started running down the block as fast as she could, the costume fairy wings she always wore flapping behind her.

Gabby's sister, Mia, and Mia's two best friends, Kate McCrady and Lainey Winters, looked at each other and laughed. They weren't going to race anywhere. It was hot and they were tired after a day of swimming. Lainey had recently conquered her fear of the water, so the girls had decided to go to the community pool to celebrate. They'd done cannonballs, stood on their hands underwater, and competed in mermaid races.

"I can't wait to go back to Never Land tomorrow," said Mia.

"Me neither," said Kate and Lainey at the exact same time. They grinned at each other. "Jinx!"

That summer, the girls had discovered that they could travel to Never Land and visit their fairy friends in Pixie Hollow whenever they wanted by walking into Gabby's closet. But the past couple of days had been packed with summertime activities, and they hadn't been able to slip away. As much fun as it had been, they were eager to get back to the magical land of the fairies.

Gabby had arrived at the end of the block and was now circling back. "You're *all* rotten eggs!" she exclaimed.

"I guess we are," Kate said with a laugh.

As they passed Maple Street, Gabby's eyes suddenly lit up. "Let's go home this way instead," she said. She grabbed her big sister's hand and pulled her along.

"Past Swensen's Sweets?" Mia asked. "Sounds good to me!"

Swensen's was an old-fashioned ice cream parlor, serving all kinds of frozen treats.

"What do you want, Gabby?" Mia asked as they stood in front of the ice cream case.

She searched her pockets for the money her mother had given her that morning.

Gabby studied the menu on the wall. "I'll take the Kitchen Sink," she said.

The other girls laughed. So did the server, a tall, freckled boy with red hair peeking out from under his paper cap. The Kitchen Sink was a gigantic dessert with twenty scoops of ice cream, every sauce you could think of, tons of whipped cream and sprinkles, and a gazillion cherries. Whenever someone ordered it, the server honked a big brass horn.

Mia finally found the ten-dollar bill. "Maybe another time," she told her sister. "Today we only have enough money for one cone each."

After much discussion, the girls placed

their orders—rainbow sherbet for Gabby, strawberry shortcake for Mia, peanut butter brickle for Lainey, and chocolate chocolate chip for Kate. When Mia lingered behind to grab some extra napkins, her eyes fell on a flyer with a half-filled volunteer sign-up sheet underneath:

Come join your neighbors for a
SUMMER BLOCK PARTY
Food! Games! Bounce House! Pet Spa!
Face Painting! Music! Raffle!
Crafts Table!
This Saturday starting at noon
(All proceeds to benefit
the Davis family)

Meghan Davis went to their school. There had recently been a fire at her

family's house, and they needed help to replace their belongings. Mia shook her head. She couldn't even imagine how hard things were for Meghan and her family and how sad they must feel.

"Hey, everyone, look at this," she said, pointing to the flyer. "We should sign up."

Kate scanned the list. "Games, that's all me," she decided, writing down her name.

"I'm going to volunteer for the pet spa!" said Lainey, grabbing the sign-up pen from Kate.

Next, Gabby wrote her name on the sheet, under Face Painting.

But Mia just stood there, looking at the list, her ice cream cone forgotten in her hand. She would have joined Kate with Games, but all those slots had been filled. Grooming pets wasn't really her thing. And none of the remaining choices—Setup, Food, Bake Sale, Raffle, Crafts Table, and Cleanup—jumped out at her, either.

"Hurry up!" said Gabby, dancing around impatiently. She had already finished her ice cream.

Mia grabbed the pen and scribbled her name under the first open space.

Lainey peered at the list. "Bake Sale?"

she said. "I didn't know you liked to bake."

Mia shrugged. "I'll figure something out," she said.

But on the walk home, Mia had a sudden stab of doubt. *Maybe I should go back,* she thought. *I'll sign up for the Crafts Table instead.*

She was about to ask the girls to turn around when a voice said, "Hey, guys!"

It was coming from the Taylors' house. Tina and Tara Taylor were standing at the front gate. Their long, straight blond hair was pulled back into matching ponytails. The girls were a year older than Mia and were identical twins. They always dressed exactly alike.

"Whatcha doing?" one of the twins asked.

"We just signed up to volunteer at the block party," Gabby piped in.

"Us too," said the other twin. "We're going to do the Bake Sale."

"So is Mia!" Gabby exclaimed.

"But I'm not—" Mia started to say.

"We're making Death by Chocolate Cake," said one twin, cutting her off.

Her sister elbowed her in the side. "No, Tina! We're making lemon meringue pie!"

"Wrong!" said Tina. "We decided on chocolate for sure." She eyed Mia. "What are *you* making?"

"Um . . . I don't know," Mia said.

"Well, I bet we'll sell more than you," said Tara. Mia smiled despite herself. The Taylor twins weren't just competitive with each other, they were competitive with everyone else, too.

"Wanna make a bet?" asked Tina.

"Actually, I—" Mia started to say.

"Sure, we'll make a bet with you," Kate interrupted.

Mia shook her head at Kate. But Kate ignored her. "Mia's going to beat you both, no problem," she added.

The twins whispered back and forth. Then they both nodded.

"Okay, Mia, if you lose you have to wear a T-shirt all week that says TARA AND TINA TAYLOR ARE THE BEST BAKERS ON SPRUCE STREET," said Tara.

"*Tina* and Tara," said Tina.

"And if . . . I mean, *when* Mia wins," Kate retorted, "you both have to wear a T-shirt that says MIA VASQUEZ IS THE BEST BAKER ON SPRUCE STREET."

"Sure," Tina said with a smirk.

Mia and her friends started to walk away. "May the best baker win!" one of the twins called after them.

"Kate! Why did you do that?" Mia asked when they were out of earshot.

"Well, somebody had to take them down a peg," said Kate. "I can't stand how they're always whispering. They act like they're better than everyone else."

"But I can't win the bet. I don't know the first thing about baking!" said Mia. She had butterflies in her stomach. How in the world was she going to pull this off?

Chapter 2

"That was delicious," said a caterpillar-shearing-talent fairy named Nettle, pushing her chair back from the table in the Home Tree tearoom. "You really do make the best poppy puff rolls, Dulcie."

"Glad you liked them," the baking-talent fairy Dulcie said absently. She took the last sip of her blackberry tea, then put down her cup. At once, a cleaning-talent fairy plucked it away. Dulcie hardly noticed. She was too busy thinking about the dessert. She had dozens of perfectly ripe raspberries and wanted to use them in something special.

"So what are you making for dessert tonight?" Nettle asked, interrupting her thoughts.

Dulcie was often asked this question, and she usually didn't answer. She liked her desserts to be a surprise. But she knew Nettle had a huge sweet tooth.

Dulcie smiled. She had it. "White almond layer cakes with raspberry filling and vanilla buttercream frosting," she said.

Nettle's eyes lit up. "Wonderful!"

Dulcie went down to the kitchen beneath the Home Tree. She put on her favorite apron and the poufy hat she always wore. Then she got to work.

The kitchen was crowded with cooking-talent fairies preparing for the next meal, but Dulcie was in her own world. She measured out flour in acorn caps. She scooped freshly churned butter from a cool stone barrel. She sprinkled in a pinch of this and added a handful of that. A feeling of peace came over her as she worked. A fairy was happiest when she was performing her talent.

At last, Dulcie slid the cakes into the oven, adding twigs to the fire. As the cakes baked, she flew outside for fresh air.

Catching a glimpse of Lily's colorful garden, she had a brilliant idea. She would put a candied flower on top of each of the cakes!

Lily was a garden-talent fairy, and her garden was two frog leaps away from the

Home Tree. As Dulcie got closer, she could hear the buzz of bumblebees.  The bees were collecting pollen from many different flowers—honeysuckle, wild roses, wisteria.

Lily was busy digging in the dirt when Dulcie approached her. "Dulcie! What a pleasant surprise," she said. "How can I help you?"

Dulcie explained about the candied flowers.

Lily leaned on the handle of her spade. "What a lovely idea!" She thought for a moment. "Here's what's in bloom. I've got tasty nasturtiums, some very pretty pansies, Johnny jump-ups, violets, yellow roses . . ."

"Pansies, please," Dulcie said. Their

smiling faces would be the perfect top-ping for her cakes.

"How many do you need?" Lily asked.

Dulcie thought about it. "I'll take ten," she decided.

Lily took her shears out of her pocket and headed over to a patch of purple and yellow pansies. When she was done cut-ting, she looked at the pile. "I gave my last basket to Dewberry. But I have another one in my house. I'll be right back."

"I'll go with you," said Dulcie.

Lily lived in a hollowed-out mushroom on one of the Home Tree's branches. Just as they reached her door, someone called out, "Yoo-hoo, Dulcie!"

Dulcie turned around. It was Marla, a cooking talent. "There you are! Do you have a moment?" she asked.

"Go ahead. I'll be out in a flash," said Lily, disappearing through her front door.

"We can't find the hazelnuts," Marla said. "Do you know where they are?"

"I'm pretty sure they're behind the barrel of sweet buttercup nectar," said Dulcie. "Otherwise, you can . . ."

Her voice trailed off as a shadow passed over them. Dulcie looked up, shading her eyes from the sun.

A hawk was flying overhead. Dulcie shrank back against the side of Lily's house. Her heart skipped a beat. A hungry hawk would snatch up a fairy in an instant.

Then Dulcie saw that the hawk already had something clutched in its talons—a wriggling fish. The hawk was struggling to hold it. With a shriek, the hawk suddenly dropped its prey.

Dulcie gasped. The fish was falling right toward them!

She grabbed Marla's hand and they scrambled out of the way. The fish crashed into Lily's house, tail first. Its head stuck out of the mushroom roof. Its mouth opened and closed silently.

"Lily!" Dulcie shouted.

She ran to the house. But just as she reached it, the door opened. Lily stepped out, blinking in confusion. Dulcie hugged her with relief.

"I was closing my closet door when I heard a big crash," the garden fairy said. "I turned around and there was a fish in my bedroom! What happened?"

"A hawk dropped a fish on your house," Marla explained.

Lily bit her lip. "Oh dear, is the fish okay?"

Just then, a team of animal-talent fairies arrived, led by Beck. They began crafting a sling out of blankets and sticks. In moments they had lifted the fish and

were taking him directly to Havendish Stream. "He'll be fine!" Beck called back to her friends.

But Lily's house was not fine. Lily and Dulcie watched as the carpenter-talent fairies arrived and studied the damage. At last, they concluded that it was beyond repair. Lily needed a new house.

"How long do you think it will take to build?" Lily asked.

"There's no telling," said a carpenter-talent fairy named Cedar. "It won't be easy to find another mushroom this size. I'll speak to Queen Clarion about where you should live in the meantime."

"Oh, Lily," said Dulcie. "I'd fly backward if I could. You wouldn't have been in your house if I hadn't asked for those flowers. You almost got squashed because of me."

"Don't be silly," said Lily. "I'm fine."

But the very thought of Lily's close call sent shivers down Dulcie's spine. As the crowd drifted away, she headed back into the Home Tree, still shaken.

Marla walked with her. "I can't even imagine how scared—" She broke off and sniffed the air. "Hey, do you smell something burning?"

Oh no! The cakes! Dulcie had completely forgotten about them. She sprinted into the kitchen, opened the oven door, and began coughing as black smoke billowed out. She groaned. Her once-perfect cakes were now smoldering charcoal bricks.

Chapter 3

Mia stood at the kitchen counter flipping through a cookbook. There were so many different recipes! Butterscotch Bars. Black Forest Cake. S'mores Cake. Red Velvet Whoopie Pies. Pineapple Upside-Down Cake . . . The choices were delicious—and endless! How would she ever pick one?

Mia slammed the cookbook shut. She glanced at the clock. Kate and Lainey would be arriving soon so they could go to Pixie Hollow. But there was still time to try out a recipe, something easy.

Mia looked over at the fishbowl on the kitchen counter. The Vasquezes were fish-sitting for their neighbors, who were on vacation. Bubbles waved his long fins at her. He was remarkably friendly for a fish, Mia thought.

"I'll make chocolate chip cookies," she told him. "Easy peasy . . . I hope."

Mia found a bag of chocolate chips in the cupboard. She placed it on the counter and began to read the directions printed on the package. The directions said to measure, mix, and drop spoonfuls of dough onto cookie sheets. How hard could that be?

"'Preheat oven to 375 degrees,'" Mia read aloud, turning the knob on the stove.

Then she tied an apron around her waist and began pulling out bowls, a hand mixer, measuring spoons, and cups.

Mia carefully measured the dry ingredients—flour, baking soda, and salt—into a bowl. Then she added butter, eggs, white sugar, brown sugar, and vanilla to another bowl.

She read the next step. "'Beat until creamy.'"

Mia plugged in the hand mixer, then realized that something was missing. "Where are those beater thingies?" she muttered. They weren't in the utensil holder or the cutlery drawer. She finally found them in the dishwasher and tried to stick them into the mixer. But why wouldn't they fit?

"It must be broken," Mia groaned. Finally, she realized she was putting them into the wrong holes. There was a left hole and a right one. Mia locked them into place.

Once the sugar, butter, and eggs were blended, Mia added the dry ingredients. She'd meant to do it a little at a time, but she accidentally dumped it in all at once.

She turned the beaters on again, sending a puff of flour into the air. The mixer shook in her hand, but Mia kept at it until the batter started to take on a creamy cookie dough consistency. She was about to dump in the chocolate chips when she thought better of it. She pictured chopped-up pieces of chocolate chips flying everywhere! She shut off the hand mixer and stirred them in by hand instead.

It was hot in the kitchen. By the time she slid the cookie sheets into the oven, she was sweating. "Baking is hard," she told Bubbles as she set the timer.

Soon the kitchen began to fill with a mouthwatering chocolatey aroma. *It won't be long now,* thought Mia.

Ding! Mia put on a pair of oven mitts and pulled out the trays,  admiring her creations. The cookies really did look—and smell—delicious.

Gabby wandered into the kitchen. Her eyes grew wide when she saw the treats. "Yum! Cookies! You made them all by yourself?" she asked.

"I did!" said Mia. "But it wasn't easy. I think they're cool enough now. Let's try one."

She picked up two still-warm cookies and handed one to her sister.

Gabby bit into the cookie. She made a horrible face and raced over to the garbage can to spit out her mouthful.

"What's the matter?" asked Mia. She

took a bite, and her mouth flooded with a salty, metallic taste. Somehow managing to swallow, she put her cookie on the counter.

"Yucky, right?" Gabby said.

Mia was confused. What had gone wrong?

The back door opened.

"Hey, guys," Kate said as she and Lainey walked into the kitchen. "Are you ready to go to . . ." Kate's voice trailed off. "Cookies!" She grabbed one.

"Don't do it!" Gabby warned.

Kate ignored her and took a huge bite. Right away she reached for a napkin to spit into. "Wow, that's salty," she said.

Mia sighed. "I don't understand. I followed the directions exactly."

Lainey picked up the empty chocolate chip package. "Did you accidentally put in too much salt?" she asked, studying the recipe on the back. "This recipe calls for one teaspoon."

Mia held up the measuring spoon. "Yeah, see? It has a big *T* on it. For teaspoon."

Lainey grimaced. "That's a tablespoon," she explained.

"I'm a disaster in the kitchen!" Mia wailed. "I'm just going to quit."

"No way!" cried Kate. "You have to beat the Taylor twins! I won't be able to live it down otherwise."

"Well, the cookies *look* amazing," said Lainey. "You're halfway there."

"But they've got to *taste* good, too," said Mia. "Let's face it, the Taylor twins are going to beat me, and I won't help raise any money for the Davises."

"Too bad you don't have the baking talent," joked Gabby.

Lainey's eyes lit up. "Mia doesn't. But we know someone who does—Dulcie! We can ask her for advice as soon as we get to Pixie Hollow."

Mia felt a small glimmer of hope. "That's a great idea!" she said. "Come on, let's go!"

The four girls were about to head upstairs when Mia's mother appeared in the kitchen doorway. "Hold it right there!" Mrs. Vasquez said. "You're not going anywhere until this mess is cleaned up."

The girls looked around the kitchen. The counter was littered with eggshells, oily butter wrappers, dirty spoons, and sticky bowls.

With a sigh Mia tossed the cookies into the garbage and rolled up her sleeves. Even with her friends' help, this was going to take a while!

Chapter 4

"There," said Dulcie as she finished drizzling melted chocolate on the last cream puff. She hoisted the platter of puffs onto her shoulder and made her way outside. Fairies and sparrow men were cleaning up the remains of Lily's mushroom house. Dulcie walked around, offering cream puffs to everyone. Funny—none of the fairies were rushing up to grab one, like they usually did.

She paused for a moment and forced

herself to take a look at Lily's house. The roof had completely collapsed and the walls had started to sag. Fairies were removing the last of Lily's belongings— her pollen collection and camellia pillows. They placed them on the grass beside the rest of her things.

Many fairies in Pixie Hollow were pitching in to help. Dulcie was lending a hand by doing what she did best—making tasty desserts. The workers needed to keep up their spirits and energy, she reasoned. And being busy in the kitchen helped her take her mind off the disaster.

"More desserts?" Cedar asked, without enthusiasm.

"Cream puffs," Dulcie said, holding out the platter.

"Maybe later. You can just put it over there with the rest," she said, pointing to a nearby table, which was covered with platters of cakes, turnovers, cookies, and muffins that Dulcie had baked.

"Do you think there's enough for everyone?" Dulcie asked.

Cedar chuckled. "Oh, I don't think you need to worry about that."

Dulcie scanned the table. Her sharp eyes noticed that a couple of treats had been taken.  "Maybe I'll just pop into the kitchen and make some more scones. . . ."

A gentle hand touched her shoulder. Dulcie turned and saw Tinker Bell. "I think maybe it's time to take a break,"

Tink said. "We have enough baked goods to last us a week."

"Or two," Vidia said, landing beside Dulcie. "Possibly even three!"

Dulcie rearranged the cream puffs, ignoring them both.

"What's going on?" a voice asked. It was a Clumsy.

Dulcie looked up and smiled. Mia, Lainey, Kate, and Gabby had entered the clearing.

The girls said hello to various fairies as they made their way over to Dulcie's table. "What's all this for?" Mia asked, looking at the tiny fairy-sized treats.

"Lily almost got squashed. And it was my fault," said Dulcie with a sigh.

"You know it wasn't," said Tink. She explained to the girls what had happened.

"Poor Lily!" exclaimed Mia. "Is she okay?"

"And poor fish!" Lainey added.

"The fish and Lily are both fine," Tink told them. "So don't worry. Now we're just cleaning up the mess."

Mia stared as a fairy lumbered by, pushing a wheelbarrow full of mushroom chunks.

"Maybe they'll be able to build Lily's new house out of cakes and muffins," said Vidia. "I mean, look at this towering table of treats right in the middle of everything."

"If the fairies can't come to the dining room, the dining room will come to them," Dulcie explained, glaring at Vidia.

"It does seem like a lot of treats," Mia said.

"I can't stop thinking about that fish crashing into Lily's house," Dulcie said. "Baking is the only thing that takes my mind off it."

"I think I have a solution," Mia said. She told the fairy all about the block party and the bake sale and the Taylor twins. "I need some help, and you could

use a change of scenery. Why don't you come back with us?"

Dulcie hesitated. "I'd like to help you, Mia," she said. "But I'm needed here."

Tink spoke up. "Dulcie, we have enough baked goods. But Lily needs a place to stay, and if you're not here she can—"

"Sleep in my room while hers is being built!" Dulcie suddenly realized, cutting her off. "But are you sure I won't be more helpful here?"

"I'm positive," said Tink.

The thought that she could help Lily made Dulcie feel better for the first time since the disaster. She was also excited at the thought of a trip to the mainland.

"If you stay until Saturday, you can come to our block party," said Gabby.

Dulcie brightened even more. "A party sounds wonderful," she said. "I'll be back in a minute." A couple of days away could be just what she needed. She flew off to pack her bags.

Chapter 5

"This is amazing!" Dulcie exclaimed as she looked around the Vasquezes' kitchen. She goggled at all the appliances and cooking tools.

Mia grinned. "Just you wait," she told her. She opened a drawer and pulled out cookie cutters in different shapes and sizes.

Dulcie lifted a flower cutter that was nearly as big as she was. Picking up another, she asked, "Is this a frog? What

will you Clumsies—I mean, humans—
think up next!"

Gabby set out a series of measuring
cups on the counter. Dulcie flew from
one to the next. She sat inside the one-
cup size and pretended to wash her hair.
"This would make a wonderful bathtub!"
she said. "What else have you got?"

Lainey presented her with measuring
spoons, whisks, and spatulas. Kate placed
a rolling pin on the counter. Dulcie
jumped on top of it and ran in place until
it spun away.

"Whew!" she said. "This is going to be
so much fun!"

"So what do you think we should make
for the block party?" Mia asked.

Dulcie sat on the edge of a muffin
tin, her legs dangling over the side. She

thought for a moment. "Well, you can't go wrong with Never Berry Pie," she said.

"But we don't have Never Berries here," said Lainey.

"What's the most delicious dessert you've made recently?" Mia asked Dulcie.

"That's easy. White almond layer cakes with raspberry filling and vanilla buttercream frosting," said Dulcie. "Each cake was going to be topped with a candied pansy. But I forgot the cakes in the oven when the fish fell on Lily's house."

"I wish I could have tried one," Lainey said.

"Let's make them for the bake sale!" Mia suggested.

Dulcie smiled and began to list all of the ingredients from memory. Mia wrote a shopping list. "I used up the butter and flour and eggs for my cookies," she said. "So we'll have to get more. And we need milk."

"Milk is easy. Where do you keep your dairy mice?" asked Dulcie.

Kate let out a loud laugh.

"Things are different here," Mia explained. "Most people don't grow their own food. We get it from this big place called a grocery store."

Dulcie's eyes widened. "Everything you need in one place?" she asked. "How strange! I can't wait to see it. Let's go!"

*

At the grocery store entrance, Mia grabbed a shopping cart. Gabby immediately climbed onto the front and hung on. Dulcie peeked out of the top of Mia's pocket. She gasped as the door slid open and a blast of cold air greeted them.

"Look at all the food!" she squealed.

Without a word of warning she darted out of Mia's pocket and began zigzagging around the produce aisle.

While Mia placed containers of fresh raspberries into her cart, Dulcie zipped over to the cucumbers. Then she swooped down to check out the tomatoes. She seemed fascinated by all the different types of lettuce. She reached out to touch the shiny purple skin of an eggplant.

She flew back to the girls. "I've never seen anything like it! How does it all get here?"

Lainey thought for a minute. "That's a good question. I'm not exactly sure. I think they get deliveries from different . . ."

But Dulcie wasn't listening. "Oranges!" she cried, zipping off.

She flew to the tippity top of a pyramid of oranges.

"Dulcie, be care—" Mia started to say.

The mountain of oranges collapsed, sending the fruit bouncing all over the floor. Dulcie darted into the air.

"Whoops!" she called as the girls chased after the oranges.

Dulcie settled down a bit after that. The fairy even managed to contain her excitement in the canned foods aisle and at the deli counter. But the baking goods aisle got her going again. All those boxes of sugar—and the spices! She flew over to study them.

"'Cream of tartar,'" she read. "'Celery salt.' I've never heard of some of these. Wait till the other baking fairies hear about this! They'll all want to visit."

"Mmm," said Mia, thinking that one fairy in the grocery store was plenty.

They headed down the frozen foods aisle. Gabby jumped off the cart and threw open a freezer door. "We're out of ice pops," she

said, grabbing one of the colorful boxes.

"Sorry, Gabby. I only have enough money to buy bake sale ingredients."

Gabby clutched the box to her chest. "Are you sure Mami didn't give you enough money for ice pops?"

"Yes, please put them back." Mia turned toward Dulcie. "Let's go get the—" She stopped and looked around. "Hey! Where did she go?"

The girls ran up and down the aisle. No Dulcie.

"Maybe she went back to the baking aisle?" Lainey suggested.

Gabby suddenly pointed to the freezer case. "There she is!"

A clear spot had been rubbed into the foggy glass. Dulcie stood on a box of frozen waffles, waving frantically.

Shaking her head, Mia opened the door. The fairy flew out.

"The door was open, and I was curious. I fl-fl-flew in!" Dulcie said, her teeth chattering. "Then the door sl-sl-slammed shut. It was fr-fr-fr-freezing! What's next?"

In the dairy aisle, Mia grabbed two cartons of eggs. Then she remembered that her father had told her to always check to make sure none were broken.

As she was examining the eggs, she heard Kate say, "Dulcie's gone again!"

"There she is," said Lainey, pointing down the aisle. "Over in the cheese case."

Dulcie was examining a large piece of Swiss. At that moment, a woman in a red sweatshirt walked over to the display.

"Dulcie, watch out!" yelled Gabby.

But Dulcie's back was turned and she didn't hear her. As the girls watched, the woman grabbed the very cheese Dulcie was standing on! She placed it in her shopping cart and headed down the aisle and around the corner.

"Why didn't Dulcie fly out of the cart?" Kate asked.

"She must have gotten trapped somehow," said Mia. "We've got to help her!"

"Let's split up!" suggested Kate.

Kate went left. Gabby and Lainey went right. Mia pushed their cart to the front of the store by the checkout lanes and peered down each aisle as she passed by.

Just then, she spotted a flash of red in the beverage aisle. She steered the cart, wheels squeaking wildly, around the few shoppers in her way and followed the woman down the next aisle. When the woman stopped to reach for a jar of salsa on a high shelf, Mia leaned in close to her cart.

She lifted a bunch of bananas. "Dulcie, where are you?" she hissed.

Dulcie sprang out and slipped into Mia's pocket.

Glancing up, Mia saw the woman gazing at her curiously.

"That's my cart, dear," the woman said.

"Oh, sorry," Mia said, replacing the bananas back in the cart.

"Don't worry," the woman said. "Happens to me all the time. Why, last week I almost accidentally bought someone else's groceries!"

"Yeah," said Mia. "I hate when that

happens. Happy shopping!" She headed off with a wave.

"Whew!" said Dulcie. "Thanks, Mia. That was a close one. Death by banana!"

"I think that woman thought I *was* bananas," Mia said.

Gabby, Kate, and Lainey showed up, out of breath.

"Did you find her?" asked Gabby.

Dulcie popped her head out of Mia's pocket and smiled.

Everyone was ready to go home. The girls split up to track down the last items on the list, then got into the shortest checkout line.

Of course, it also happened to be the slowest.

"Hi, Mia," said a voice behind her. She spun around. It was the Taylor twins. Mia hoped Dulcie would remember to keep herself hidden. She placed her hand over the top of her pocket, just in case.

Tara peered into Mia's cart. "Raspberries, huh?" she said. "I bet you're making raspberry cheesecake."

Mia shook her head.

"Raspberry turnovers?" suggested the other twin.

"That's not it," said Gabby.

"I know!" said Tara. "Raspberry thumbprint cookies!"

"Wrong again," said Kate. "You're just going to have to wait to find out."

"May the best dessert win," said Tina.

"It will," said a small voice from inside Mia's pocket. "Ours!"

Tina leaned forward. "What did you just say?" she asked Mia.

"Nothing," said Mia quickly. "I just wanted to wish you both good luck tomorrow."

Tina and Tara looked at her suspiciously and switched lanes, whispering to each other.

"Oh, I hope you beat those two," said Kate, shaking her head.

The line started to move, and soon they were packed up and ready to go.

"What a trip," said Dulcie on the walk home. "Everything about the grocery store was so fantastic. Except for the baked goods." She yawned. "Did you see those cupcakes wrapped in plastic?"

And then she fell asleep, right in Mia's pocket.

Chapter 6

Dulcie woke up bright and early on Friday morning in the comfortable bed in Mia's dollhouse. She yawned and stretched, then looked over at Mia. The girl was sound asleep, her pillow over her head.

"Rise and shine!" Dulcie cried. "It's baking day!"

Mia just rolled over.

Dulcie flew downstairs. She found Gabby sitting at the kitchen counter eating a bowl of Sugar Os.

"Are you hungry?" asked Gabby.

"Does a bunny hop?" Dulcie replied. When Gabby looked confused, she added, "In fairy terms, that means yes."

Gabby ran upstairs to grab a tiny bowl and spoon from the dollhouse. Mia still wasn't awake. Once back downstairs, Gabby discovered that only a single Sugar O would fit in the bowl. She added a few drops of milk and placed the bowl in front of the fairy.

Dulcie gobbled it up.

After breakfast, Gabby pulled out mixing bowls, large spoons, and cake pans of all shapes and sizes.

"These are gigantic!" said Dulcie, flying over to examine a sheet cake pan. She thought for a minute. "They're perfect!"

"What's perfect?" said Mia, who had finally made her way downstairs.

"Fly with you, Mia," Dulcie said. "I found these big cake pans. Why don't we make a couple of sheet cakes? That way we can get the most slices."

Mia eyed the long pans nervously. "I guess I was imagining something, well, smaller. I've never baked anything but cookies, you know."

"Don't worry. I'll help you," Dulcie said.

Mia nodded. "I want your help. But I also want to win fair and square. I have to do the baking."

Dulcie agreed. "The best part of baking is seeing your own creation. I'll stay out of the way." She settled herself on top of the blender, where she could oversee everything—and call out instructions.

"First, melt some butter!" Dulcie instructed.

Mia looked around uncertainly.

"Stove. Pan. Butter. Go!" Dulcie explained.

Mia pulled out the butter and a saucepan and got to work.

"Yes, that's good, keep stirring. Lovely! Now, take a pastry brush and cover the bottom and the sides of the pans with a thin coating of butter."

Mia looked up. "What's a pastry brush?"

"No pastry brush?" Dulcie said.

"I have a new paintbrush I haven't used yet," offered Gabby from her perch at the counter.

"Perfect!" said Dulcie with a sigh of relief.

After the paintbrush was washed and dried, Mia went to work. Dulcie watched. "Remember, I said a *thin* coating," she called out. "That's much too thick. Here, let me show you."

Dulcie flew down to the counter. She grabbed the paintbrush and managed to dip it in the saucepan. But when she hoisted the large brush, heavy with melted butter, over her shoulder, she lost her balance.

"Oh . . . oh . . . oh . . . ," she cried as she skidded from one end of the slippery surface to the other on her bottom. When she stood up, butter dripped from her dress.

Mia laughed. "Well, that's one way to butter a pan."

"Ha ha," said Dulcie. "Keep buttering. *Thinly.* I'll be back in a minute."

Upstairs in the dollhouse, Dulcie opened her little suitcase. She changed her clothes quickly, then flew back to the kitchen. Next, she taught Mia how to measure dry ingredients exactly, by leveling off the top of her measuring cups and spoons with the straight edge of a butter knife.

"You need to be very precise when you bake," she informed her.

Mia laughed. "No need to remind me."

Mia began combining the precisely measured dry ingredients in a bowl: flour, baking powder, salt, sugar. "A little more gently," said Dulcie, as a cloud of flour dust filled the air.

Mia coughed. "Sorry," she said, and started creaming the butter and sugar with the mixer.

Dulcie flew over to admire the hand mixer. "What a marvelous invention!" she said.

Then Mia unscrewed the top of the vanilla extract. "No, we need almond, not vanilla," Dulcie said, darting forward. It was so hard to just sit and watch. She wanted to bake!

But she soon discovered that while she could hold an empty measuring spoon, lifting one filled with liquid was not quite so easy.

"Whoa . . . whoa . . . whoa!" she shouted, trying to balance the heavy spoon.

Gabby jumped up to help, but she was too late. The spoonful of extract poured onto Dulcie's head and all over the counter.

Silently, Mia tore a strip of paper towel and handed it to Dulcie. "See you in a bit," she called as Dulcie flew back upstairs for a second outfit change.

"Now for the challenging part," Dulcie said when she returned.

Mia wiped her brow. "This all seems pretty challenging to me," she said.

"We need to add just the egg whites. They'll make the batter light and airy. So we've got to separate the yolks from the whites," said Dulcie.

Mia held up an egg. Dulcie's eyes went round.

"Oh my!" she said. "We use hummingbird eggs in Pixie Hollow. I'm glad you're handling this one."

Mia cracked the egg and poured it into her hand, allowing the white to slip through her fingers as instructed. But then the egg yolk broke and seeped into the white. It happened two more times. Dulcie wrung her hands. She didn't want to run out of eggs!

"Let's try it one more time," she said. "Fourth time's the charm!"

Mia's gaze fell on the utensil holder on the counter. Her eyes lit up and she grabbed a slotted spoon, gently cracking an egg over it. The egg white slipped through the slots into the bowl while the yolk stayed on top of the spoon.

"That was a good idea, Mia," said Dulcie. "You're really catching on."

"Thanks." Mia beamed.

"Now you need to beat the egg whites until soft peaks form," explained Dulcie. "Your mixer should make short work of it!"

Mia turned on the hand mixer. "It's working!" she said, lifting the beaters to show Dulcie. Unfortunately, she didn't remember to turn it off first. Dulcie was covered with frothy egg whites.

"Sorry, Dulcie," she said.

"No problem," said Dulcie, wiping her eyes. She stayed to instruct Mia how to fold the egg whites into the cake mixture. Then she headed back upstairs to change one more time.

In her dollhouse bedroom, Dulcie looked

in her suitcase and discovered that she was out of clean clothes. But then she remembered Rosetta telling her about Mia's shoe boxes of doll clothes. Dulcie easily found them in Mia's closet. Inside each box were piles of outfits, perfectly fairy sized. But which one would she choose?

When Dulcie returned downstairs, Mia was busy pouring the sweet batter into the prepared pans. Dulcie landed beside the toaster and struck a pose.

"Wow!" Gabby said, clapping.

"What do you think, Mia?" Dulcie asked.

Mia turned and burst out laughing. Dulcie was wearing a fringed vest, jean skirt, and boots with spurs. A lasso was wrapped around her waist and a tiny hat sat on her head.

"What's so funny?" Dulcie asked.

"Nothing!" said Mia, sti-
fling a giggle. "You look great
in a cowboy hat, Dulcie."

Dulcie checked her reflection in the
side of the toaster. She straightened her
hat. "I do, don't I?" she said.

Mia slid the pans into the oven. She
set the timer. While the cakes baked, the
kitchen filled with the delicious aroma of
almonds.

Mia and Gabby sat down at the kitchen
table and played a game of Go Fish as they
waited for the cakes to be done. Dulcie
flew from one sister's shoulder to the
other's to check out their hands.

"If I were you, I would—" she started to
say to Gabby.

"Dulcie, that's cheating!" Mia protested.

"Oops!" said Dulcie.

"Something smells good!" said Mrs. Vasquez as she passed through the kitchen on her way outside.

Ding! Mia, Dulcie, and Gabby all jumped up, eager to see how Mia's creation had turned out this time.

Mia opened the oven door and stepped back from the heat.

"Grab some oven mitts and slide out the rack," Dulcie instructed. "Now take a dried pine needle and stick it in the middle of the cake."

Mia gave her a look. "I think I'll try a toothpick," she said. She grabbed a toothpick from the counter and stuck it into one of the cakes. It came out clean.

Dulcie declared that the golden-brown

cakes were perfect. Mrs. Vasquez came back into the kitchen and took a look.

"You did this all by yourself, Mia?" she asked in surprise. "I am so impressed! I had no idea we had such a talented baker in the family." She fanned herself. "It's hot in here, isn't it? How about I turn on the sprinkler in the backyard? You two could put on your suits and cool off."

She didn't need to ask twice. Mia and Gabby went to their rooms and changed into their swimsuits. As they ran through the sprinklers, Dulcie the Cowgirl watched from a nearby tree branch. Her eyes wandered around the yard.

Something was bothering her about the cakes. It felt as if something was missing.

Mia ran over, her hair soaked. "So I think we should make the raspberry filling today and then frost the cakes first thing in the morning," she said.

"All right," said Dulcie absentmindedly.

"I only wish we had some candied pansies," said Mia. "Then it would be exactly like your recipe." She shrugged. "Oh well."

Mia ran back to the sprinkler, and Dulcie sat up. That's what was missing! The finishing touch!

Just on the other side of the Vasquezes' fence Dulcie found what she was looking for—a beautiful bunch of pansies. After several trips back and forth between the yards, she had quite a pile to show Mia. Excited, she flew over to get the girls.

"Mia! Gabby! I found the best cake toppers!" Dulcie cried. "Come and see!"

Mia wrapped a beach towel around her

waist and followed Dulcie to the side of the house. Gabby was right behind her.

"Pansies!" Dulcie exclaimed. "Just like you wanted!"

Mia stared at the pile of flowers. "Where did you get these?" she asked.

"Oh, from a nearby garden patch," Dulcie replied, waving her hand toward the fence.

"Over the fence?" Gabby asked.

"Yes!" said Dulcie. "Aren't they beautiful?"

Mia groaned. "Mrs. Peavy is going to kill me!"

"Mrs. Who?" asked Dulcie.

"Mrs. Peavy," answered Gabby. "She lives next door. She's really grumpy."

"What should I do?" Mia muttered. "Play dumb? Or apologize?"

Dulcie was confused. Didn't flowers belong to everyone?

She watched as Mia ran into the house and came back out wearing a sundress. "I'm going to apologize," Mia told them. She marched off to her neighbor's house.

Dulcie and Gabby followed. When no one answered the doorbell, they went through the side gate and found Mrs. Peavy standing in her garden, frowning at her patch of pansies. Instead of a bounty of smiling yellow and purple faces, there were just stems.

Not so long ago, Mia had accidentally trampled a few of Mrs. Peavy's flowers and found herself stuck weeding the woman's overgrown backyard. Then Rosetta had used her fairy magic to transform it into a well-tended garden. Now Mrs. Peavy thought that Mia had the greenest thumb in town.

"Well, hello, Mia," she said.

Mia gulped. "Hi, Mrs. Peavy."

"Someone picked all of my pansies!" said Mrs. Peavy. "Who would do such a thing?"

"Oh, Mrs. Peavy, I'm so sorry," Mia said. "A friend is visiting me from, um, a foreign land. She didn't realize you can't pick flowers from other people's gardens. She's the one who took your pansies."

Mrs. Peavy narrowed her eyes. "That's unacceptable, Mia," she said.

This was not going well at all.

Dulcie lighted on Mia's shoulder. "Tell her they're for the block party!" she whispered in her ear.

"Well, um, we were planning to candy

them and put them on slices of cake for the bake sale at the block party tomorrow," explained Mia. "You know, for the Davis family."

"I don't care what they're for. It's stealing, plain and simple. I have half a mind to . . ." Mrs. Peavy waved her hand. "Just go. It's too late now, they're already picked. There's nothing you can do."

"I—I'm sorry, Mrs. Peavy," Mia stammered.

She let herself out the gate. Dulcie and Gabby hurried after her.

"I'd fly backward if I could," Dulcie said.

Mia wanted to look stern. But she couldn't stay mad at the earnest-looking fairy in the cowgirl outfit. "I know, pardner, I know."

Chapter 7

At Mia's house, everything was falling into place. The cakes had cooled and slipped easily from the pans. They sat on wire racks on the counter, golden and moist. The raspberry filling was delicious. It would be spread between cake layers in the morning. Then the cakes would be iced and cut into slices.

All four girls had made the candied pansies together that afternoon. Dulcie had watched with pride as Mia expertly separated the egg whites with her slotted spoon trick. Kate had beaten the egg whites and added some water. Then she, Mia, and Lainey had painted the flowers with the mixture.

"Now it's time to add the sugar!" said Dulcie.

Gabby carefully sprinkled each flower with superfine sugar.

"They're beautiful," said Mia.

Dulcie stood at the end of the counter, admiring their work. "Every recipe needs a pinch of magic," she said to Mia.

That night, when it was time for bed, Dulcie pulled on her nightgown and settled under the covers. Mia crawled into her own bed. Almost immediately, her breathing became deep and steady.

How can she fall asleep so quickly? Dulcie wondered as she tossed and turned.

Then her mind landed on slicing the cakes. Sliced pieces didn't seem special enough. What could she do to make them unique?

Dulcie slipped out from under the covers and flew downstairs to the quiet kitchen. As she paced the countertop, thinking, she spied a half-open drawer and peeked inside. There they were—the cookie cutters she had admired earlier. She studied several—a rabbit, a man with a beard and a funny hat, a pumpkin. She selected a small circle and a star.

Will Mia like this idea? she asked herself. *Of course she will!*

Dulcie went straight to work. Placing the round cookie cutter on the first sheet cake, she pressed down, cutting out a perfect circle. She did this over and over until she had dozens of cutout cake circles. With the star-shaped cookie cutter, she did the same to the second cake. Then she coated the top of each circle with raspberry filling. Last, she stacked the stars on top.

When she was done, she flew up and looked down on her creations. Dozens of miniature cakes. They looked elegant. And delicious. And positively magical.

From the corner of her eye, she saw Bubbles staring at her from his tank. He was waving a fin at her. She landed on the counter next to his bowl.

"Perfect, right?" she asked him. "You can tell me the truth, Fish."

Fish . . .

. . . mushroom . . .

. . . Lily, Dulcie thought.

She had managed to push the acci-
dent out of her mind during her visit to
the mainland. But now her worries came
flooding back. Did Lily have a new house
yet? Had the fairies run out of baked
goods? She felt an urge to return to Pixie
Hollow at once.

She would miss the block party. But all Mia would have to do in the morning was frost the little cakes and top them with the flowers.

Dulcie smiled. So simple! Her work here was done. She flew back upstairs.

Balancing a pen on her shoulder, she wrote a quick note and left it on her neatly made bed. She found her clothes by the window. They'd been washed and hung out to dry on a line of string, held in place by paperclips. Now she understood why Gabby had been looking for paperclips earlier.

Dulcie changed, packed, and then snapped her clamshell suitcase closed. She hovered over Mia's ear.

"Good luck tomorrow," she whispered. "Hope you like the cakes."

Mia turned over in her sleep.

Dulcie picked up her suitcase and flew to Gabby's room. "Thanks for washing my clothes," she whispered in the little girl's ear.

Then Dulcie headed to the closet. As soon as she entered, she felt a warm breeze. The smell of orange blossoms and clover filled the air. She closed her eyes and smiled. There was nothing like returning home.

Chapter 8

"Rise and shine, Dulcie!" said Mia.

There was no answer.

"Up and at 'em," she called. "We have cakes to frost!"

Still no answer.

Mia walked over to the dollhouse and peered into Dulcie's bedroom. The room was spotless, as if no one had ever stayed there. She looked closely. A piece of paper the size of a postage stamp was sitting on the pillow.

Mia plucked it up and laid it in her hand. The writing was so tiny! She rummaged around in her desk drawer until she found a magnifying glass. She held it up to the note and read:

Dear Mia,

I have to go back to Pixie Hollow and make sure Lily is doing okay. I hope you like what I did with the cakes! Good luck.

Love, Dulcie

Mia got a funny feeling in her stomach. What about their plan? The one that involved Dulcie being there to guide her every step of the way? And what had Dulcie done with the cakes?

Mia padded downstairs. Her parents

sat at the kitchen table drinking their morning coffee.

"You must have been up late last night, *mija*," her father said, looking up from the newspaper. "But your little cakes look great."

"Such a lovely idea," added her mother. "But it's going to be a lot of work frosting them. I wish we could help, but we have to be at the block party in fifteen minutes!"

Little cakes? What were her parents talking about? Mia looked over at the kitchen counter and gasped.

There sat row after row of tiny cakes. Mia saw the two cookie cutters sitting on the counter and realized what Dulcie had done.

The cakes were very cute. But there

were so many of them! Without Dulcie's help, how could she get them finished in time?

And how did you even *make* frosting? Mia grabbed a cookbook and frantically flipped through the pages. But each recipe was more complicated than the last. She needed one that didn't require ten steps. Or more eggs to separate. Or a candy

thermometer. What *was* a candy thermometer, anyway?

Mia groaned and slammed the cookbook shut, just as Gabby wandered into the kitchen. "How am I ever going to do this?"

"Do what?" asked Gabby.

Mia explained her problem.

"I'll help," said Gabby. "And you know Kate and Lainey will, too."

So Mia made two emergency calls. All she had to say was "I need help."

Lainey and Kate were there in record time. Mia met them at the door.

"It's getting late," Kate informed her. "We have to be at the block party soon."

"I'm in big trouble," Mia said. "Come on in." She showed them the little cakes.

"Whoa!" said Kate. "That's a lot of cakes to frost!"

"And I have no idea how to make frosting!" Mia wailed.

Lainey thought for a minute. "My mom sometimes uses the recipe on a box of powdered sugar. Do you have any?"

She did! Mia pulled a box down from the cupboard and read the recipe quickly. All she needed was powdered sugar, butter, vanilla, and milk. Easy!

There wasn't a moment to lose. She unwrapped the butter, sifted the sugar, and added the vanilla and milk. Then she began to blend the ingredients. The butter was hard, and she had to hold on to the mixer with both hands. Chunks of butter flew everywhere.

Mia turned off the mixer and peered into the bowl.

"Does this seem right?" she asked.

Lainey frowned. "Um, it's supposed to look creamy," she said. "This looks kind of . . . gloppy."

Mia stuck a knife into the frosting and smeared it on one of the tiny cakes. It slid right off, leaving an oily trail.

"Yuck," said Mia. She put her head in her hands. "I give up."

Kate studied the recipe. "It says here that the butter should be softened," she said. "I don't think it was soft when you blended it."

"I'm kind of in a rush here," said Mia. "So I skipped that part. Now how am I going to fix it?"

"Can we start over?" Lainey asked.

"I'm out of butter," Mia said. "And sugar." She looked at the clock. "And time."

Gabby dragged over the stepstool and peered into the bowl. "Super yuck," she said.

Mia sighed. "You're not helping."

Gabby thought for a minute. "Well, if the butter was too cold, why don't you just heat it up?" she asked with a shrug.

Mia looked at her sister. Maybe she was on to something. "How would we heat it?" she asked.

"Put it on the stove?" suggested Gabby.

"I think that will cook it," Lainey replied.

"Put the bowl on top of a hot water bottle?" Kate offered.

Mia thought for a minute, then shook her head. "No, I think that will melt it. We need a gentle way to heat it. Something we can turn off easily . . ."

Suddenly, she had it! She ran upstairs to the bathroom and returned with . . .

"A hair dryer!" Kate said. "Mia, that's genius!"

Kate turned the dryer on the lowest setting and aimed it the bowl. Lainey turned the bowl, and Mia mixed. Within minutes the frosting had transformed. It was now smooth and creamy.

Gabby tasted it. "Delicious!" she declared. They all started frosting the cakes.

Every time Mia finished one, it seemed as if ten more took its place. She was sure

they were never going to finish. As each cake was frosted, Gabby carefully placed a delicate candied flower on top.

Finally, they were done. The girls stared at the cakes, which covered every inch of the kitchen counter.

"They're beautiful," said Kate.

"Amazing," said Lainey.

"They're fairy cakes!" said Gabby.

"And they're done," Mia said with a tired grin.

Chapter 9

"*Beep! Beep!* Fairy cakes coming through!" Gabby announced. She led the way down the street to the bake sale stand. People turned and smiled at the little girl in her fairy wings and tutu. In honor of the block party, Gabby was also wearing a plastic jeweled tiara. Kate and Lainey followed closely behind. Mia followed, too, carrying two big plates full of little cakes.

When they reached the blocked-off street, it was full of people running around making last-minute preparations.

A rainbow of balloons arched over a stage where a band was setting up. "Testing. One, two, three," a musician said into the microphone.

The bounce house was inflated. Folding tables had been decorated for all the different activities. Hamburgers, hot dogs, and sausages were cooking on the grills. A clown arrived carrying a bag filled with balloons ready to be twisted into swords, flowers, and a whole zoo of animals.

The tables at the bake sale stand were nearly full with treats. Mia, Lainey, and Kate stood looking for a place to put the plates.

"Good morning, Mia," said Ms. Choi,

a fellow volunteer. "Why don't you set up over there?" She pointed to a small, rickety-looking table.

"Can you take it from here, Mia?" asked Kate. "We've got to go to our booths now. We're all on first shift."

Mia nodded.

Gabby tugged Lainey's hand. "Take me to the face-painting booth," she said.

Mia frowned. "Take me to the face-painting booth what?"

"Now?" suggested Gabby.

Lainey and Mia shook their heads.

Gabby laughed. "I know, I know. Please!" she said.

"Okay," said Lainey, taking Gabby's hand. They went off in one direction and Kate went in the other.

"Hey, Mia!" called Mrs. Funkhauser, another volunteer. "These are my famous Secret Kiss cupcakes. There's a surprise inside each one. Can you guess what it is? A chocolate kiss!" she said before Mia could answer.

Mr. Duncan, a retired man who lived on the next block, pointed proudly to his creation. "Snickerdoodles!" he said.

"We made truffle brownies," said Tina Taylor.

"And we already sold three of them!" added Tara. "Better catch up!"

Mia smiled at everyone and set her plates on the table next to the others. The table was wobbly.

"What did you make?" asked Tina.

"Fairy cakes!" said Mia.

The twins frowned. "Fairy what?"

"Oh my. What a perfectly darling name," said Ms. Choi. "You had better be careful, Mia. That table isn't very—"

Bang! The table suddenly collapsed.

"—stable," Ms. Choi finished. "Oh no."

Mia bent down to pick up the plates. Luckily, they hadn't broken, but several of the cakes had gotten smushed. Ms. Choi brought over two large platters. They moved the cakes onto them. Mia repositioned the candy flowers and smoothed out the frosting.

"Tough break," said Tara.

"I'm so sorry, Mia," said Ms. Choi. "We can see about getting you another table. Why don't you share with me until then?"

Mia looked at Ms. Choi's table, already crowded with cakes, plates, and napkins.

She shook her head. "It's okay. I'll think of something," she said.

What would Dulcie do? she thought.

Then she remembered something the baking talent had said in Pixie Hollow. "If they can't come to the dining room, the dining room will come to them." Dulcie had brought all the baked goods outside to feed the workers.

That's it! thought Mia. But she'd need help. She picked up the platters. "I'll be back," she said.

She hurried over to the face-painting booth. "I need your help selling the fairy cakes," she said to Gabby.

"I need your help selling the fairy cakes what?" replied Gabby.

"I need your help selling the fairy cakes, *please,*" Mia said.

"That's better. But I can't. I'm expecting my first customer any minute."

"It will only be for a little while," Mia explained. "Then you can come right back."

"Ahem."

Mia and Gabby turned around. There stood Mrs. Peavy. She looked at them sternly. "If I can part with my pansies for a good cause, I think you might be able to help your sister," she said to Gabby.

Gabby gulped. "Okay," she said.

Then, unexpectedly, Mrs. Peavy smiled. "My flowers look beautiful on your cakes, Mia," she said. "You do have such a magic touch."

"Take one," offered Mia. "On me. It's the least I can do."

"Thank you," Mrs. Peavy said. "But

I insist on paying. For the Davises." She bought two!

"And maybe Mia will let you paint her face first," she said to Gabby before she left.

Mia nodded. She set down her cakes and took a seat across from Gabby.

After painting a wobbly star on each of Mia's cheeks, Gabby stood up. "Let's start selling fairy cakes!" she said. The girls picked up the platters.

Mia called out to the crowd with all her heart, "Fairy cakes! Fairy cakes! Get your fairy cakes here!"

But she hardly needed to say a thing. As soon as people caught a glimpse of the pretty cakes, they lined up to buy them.

"Hi, Mia! I'll take three, please!" said Mr. Bergen.

"Those are the cutest cakes I've ever seen!" said Mrs. Daly.

"Mommy, Mommy, I want a fairy cake!" a little girl called.

Before they knew it, they had sold every last one.

"Thanks, Gabby," Mia told her sister. "You can go back to the face-painting booth now."

"See you!" said Gabby. She handed over her platter and scampered off.

Mia returned to the bake sale stand with the empty platters.

"So how many cakes have you sold, Mia?" Tara called out. "We've sold a whole tray of brownies already!"

Mia set down the platters. "I sold them all," she said.

The twins looked at her. "Really?" asked Tina. "You're not kidding?"

"Really," said Mia.

She was expecting the girls to be mad. But they just shrugged.

"You beat us fair and square," said Tara.

"I wish I'd gotten to try one of your cakes," said Tina. "They looked really good."

"Thanks, Tina," said Mia.

Tara sighed. "I guess we'll go have those T-shirts made up tomorrow."

Mia shook her head. "Let's forget about that. The important thing is that we raised money for the Davis family."

And that I won! she thought to herself. She glanced across the street, where the Davis family was standing onstage, looking slightly stunned at the crowd of friends and neighbors who had banded together to help them. "Sometimes it takes losing everything to make you realize how rich you really are," Mr. Davis announced.

Mia smiled. Making the fairy cakes had certainly been a lot of trouble. But it was definitely worth it.

Mia helped Ms. Choi sell pieces of her coffee cake for a while. Then she decided to explore the block party. She stopped by to check on Gabby and bought a ticket from her parents, who were now working at the raffle booth. They were pleased to hear about how quickly the cakes had sold. Next Mia went to Kate's booth. She tried the ring toss and the egg and spoon race. She didn't win either one, but she had fun.

Then she went home to get Bingo and brought him to Lainey's booth for a brushing. He put up with it until Lainey tried to tie a big red bow around his neck.

It was a wonderful day. Mia was only sorry that Dulcie wasn't there to share it with her. She would have loved every minute.

Chapter 10

"I see a rabbit!" said Lainey.

The four girls lay sideways in the Vasquezes' hammock so they could all fit. They rocked back and forth gently as they stared up at the clouds.

Kate closed one eye and cocked her head. "I don't know," she said. "Looks more like a baseball glove to me."

"You're both wrong," said Mia. "It's definitely a cupcake."

"Don't you mean a fairy cake?" said Gabby.

The girls laughed. The block party had been a huge success, lasting until long after sundown. A lot of money had been raised for the Davis family, who couldn't stop thanking their friends and neighbors.

"I can't believe you let the Taylor twins off the hook," said Kate.

Mia shrugged. "The bet just didn't seem that important. Anyway, the twins aren't so awful."

"Too bad Dulcie didn't get to taste the cakes," said Gabby. "They were so yummy!"

"I wonder if Lily's house ever got fixed," said Lainey.

"And if Dulcie is still baking like crazy," said Kate.

Mia stood up. "What are we waiting for? Let's go to Pixie Hollow right now." She ran into the house and picked up a small paper bag she'd left in the kitchen. Then she met the girls at Gabby's closet door. It creaked open. Mia took a deep breath as they all shuffled forward into the darkness. The air was heavy with the sweet smell of orange blossoms.

They stepped onto the sunny bank of Havendish Stream. Birds were chirping and chubby rabbits were hopping by. Kate, Mia, Lainey, and Gabby headed straight to the Home Tree, where they noticed a trail of fairies carrying furniture and suitcases.

"Welcome back!" said Beck, her arms filled with caterpillar wool blankets. "Lily's temporary house is finished!"

Lily waved to them excitedly and flew over. "It's a pumpkin!" she said. "It was Dulcie's idea. None of the mushrooms we found in the forest are big enough

yet, so I'm going to live in this pumpkin until one grows."

"And Dulcie's been making all kinds of pumpkin treats—scones, pies, and soups," said Cedar, who was carrying a toadstool footstool. "It's a nice break from all the cream puffs."

Dulcie flew by holding a tray. "Pumpkin turnover, anyone?" she said.

The girls sat on a small hill and watched as Lily moved into her new home. She opened one of her many windows and leaned out. "All this place needs now is some flowers!" she said.

"She's really happy," said Dulcie, settling on Mia's shoulder. "So how did you like the little cakes? Oh no! I just realized I was in such a rush to get back I forgot to leave you a frosting recipe!"

"It's okay," said Mia. "I figured it out by myself."

Lainey cleared her throat.

"I mean, we figured it out together." Mia smiled. "It was fun, actually."

"And did you beat the Taylor twins?" Dulcie asked.

"Like a rug!" offered Kate.

At Dulcie's confused expression, Mia said, "I did. But it didn't really matter."

"I understand," said Dulcie with a nod.

"I named them Fairy Cakes!" Gabby said proudly.

"Fairy Cakes!" said Dulcie. "What a lovely name! I wish I could have tried one."

Mia reached into the paper bag she had brought with her. "Surprise!"

The cake was big enough for a few of the fairies to share.

"You definitely have the baking talent, Mia," Dulcie announced, her mouth full of cake.

Mia was touched. That was a high compliment coming from the best baking-talent fairy in Pixie Hollow.

"You're a good teacher," she said.

"Next time don't wait so long to visit," said Dulcie. "We miss you when you're not here."

The girls looked at each other and smiled.

"We won't let it happen again," said Mia.

"We promise," said Gabby. Kate and Lainey nodded in agreement.

Just then, Mia remembered something. "Hey, you forgot this at my house," she said to Dulcie. She pulled the tiny cowboy hat out of the bag and plopped it onto the fairy's head.

"Ride 'em, cowgirl!" said Mia.

"Yee-haw!" shouted Dulcie.

Read the Never Girls adventure that started it all!

In a blink of an eye, four best friends all get their biggest wish—they're whisked off to Never Land, home to Tinker Bell and her fairy friends. The adventure of a lifetime is just beginning! But how will the Never Girls ever get home again?

Read another Never Girls adventure!

Lainey has never been alone in the Never Land forest before. First she thinks she hears a rabbit talking to a fox. Then she finds an underground hideout. Are the Never Girls really the only children in Never Land?